The Dragon and the Turtle

GO ON SAFARI

Donita K. Paul and Evangeline Denmark

illustrated by Vincent Nguyen

WATERBROOK
PRESS

THE DRAGON AND THE TURTLE GO ON SAFARI
PUBLISHED BY WATERBROOK PRESS
12265 Oracle Boulevard, Suite 200
Colorado Springs, Colorado 80921

The Scripture quotation is taken from the Holy Bible, New International Version®. NIV®. Copyright © 1973, 1978, 1984 by Biblica Inc.™ Used by permission of Zondervan. All rights reserved world-wide. www.zondervan.com.

The characters and events in this book are fictional, and any resemblance to actual persons or events is coincidental.

ISBN 978-0-307-44645-9

Cover design by Leslie E. Seetin and Mark D. Ford

Published in association with the literary agency of Alive Communications Inc., 7680 Goddard Street, Suite 200, Colorado Springs, CO 80920, www.alivecommunications.com.

Published in the United States by WaterBrook Multnomah, an imprint of the Crown Publishing Group, a division of Random House Inc., New York.

WATERBROOK and its deer colophon are registered trademarks of Random House Inc.

The Cataloging-in-Publication Data is on file with the Library of Congress.

Printed in the United States of America
2011—First Edition

10 9 8 7 6 5 4 3 2 1

To Elnora E. Paul, who as mother, grandmother,

great-grandmother, and Sunday school teacher,

introduced many children to the love of a good story.

Roger the turtle blew on his toasted marshmallow. "It's going to be fun spending the whole night at the base of Mount Sillymanborrow."

"I didn't know it got so dark on safari," said Padraig the dragon.

"That's why we have this fire," said Roger.

"It's a roarin' good one too." Padraig settled into his seat. "Toss me another marshmallow."

"Proper adventurers always say please," Roger teased.

"Yes, indeed. Please." Padraig speared a puffy marshmallow with a stick.

Roger searched the ground. "Padraig, my good fellow, is the box of baked bugs on your side?"

As the dragon handed over the crunchy treat, a screeching noise made him jump, hover in the air, then return to the ground with a *whump*. "My stars! What was that?"

"Not to worry, old chap. That was definitely the call of a howler monkey," Roger explained.

"Oh, righto," said Padraig. "Very loud fellows, aren't they?"

"Indeed." Roger nodded. "Now about those baked bugs."

"Oh, stinky aphids! I dropped them all over."

"I'll help you clean up."

The turtle gulped a crispy bug, then paused. "Wait! Did you hear that rustling?"

Padraig squinted into the night. "What makes leaves rattle in the tippy top of a tree?"

The boys looked at each other. "Giraffe!"

"Mount Sillymanborrow giraffes are the tallest in the world," said Roger. "If we spend the whole night, in the morning we'll get to see them and all the other animals."

Padraig grinned. "Cheerio. Right jolly good spot for us."

Roger toasted another marshmallow. "This is the best place in the world to hunt for fierce and fantastic beasts."

"Um…do we have to hunt the fierce beasts?" Padraig asked.

Roger nodded. "Fierce and fantastic! That's how our exploring team likes 'em."

"Oh." Padraig didn't sound convinced.

"I'm getting sleepy," said Roger.

Padraig didn't want to close his eyes when there were fierce animals roaming around. "I think we should do a safari dance around our campfire."

"Agreed!"

A noise interrupted their dance. The boys froze, listening to the night sounds of the jungle.

"What could have made that *thud*?" Roger asked.

"Only one animal I can think of." Padraig balanced on one foot. "An elephant. Elephants travel in herds, you know."

"In herds?" Roger's voice cracked. He wasn't sure he wanted to meet a herd of elephants in the dark.

"Maybe we should get inside the tent, just in case," Padraig suggested.

"A capital idea." Roger jumped into the safety of the tent.

Inside, Roger pulled out his flashlight and prepared his best storytelling voice. "Ahem! And now I will relate the fantastical legend of Mount Sillymanborrow. Do you want to hear the tale?"

Padraig frowned. "No. I do not."

Roger made his voice normal again. "Why not?"

"It'll be too scary."

"It's not scary at all."

"Doesn't matter." Padraig crossed his arms. "It'll be scary in the dark."

"Oh, all right." Roger pulled his head into his shell.

Padraig didn't like disappointing his friend. "You could tell it tomorrow. I'd like to hear it then."

The boys snuggled down. Not because they were tired, but because sleeping bags with shiny outsides and fluffy insides are so inviting.

Roger popped his head back out. "Exceptional thinking, old boy. The story will be even better tomorrow."

"Why?"

"Because I will have had all night to think about it."

A sound disturbed the cold night air.

"I say, Roger. Did you hear that?"

"I most certainly did, Professor Padraig."

"Why did you call me Professor?"

"Because I've decided you're the animal expert. You must have gone to school lots to learn all about jungle beasts."

"Yes," agreed Padraig. "Yes, I must have."

"So, what do you think it was, Professor Padraig?"

Padraig paused, than answered, "A rare Sumatran rhinoceros."

Roger let out a low whistle. "Great horns and hooves! Do you think it knows we're here?"

"I bet it knows our food is here," Padraig said. "Maybe we should throw some outside in case it's looking for a snack."

The boys rummaged through their gear and tossed some marshmallows, baked bugs, and graham crackers out of the tent.

"That should take care of that." Roger licked sticky marshmallow from his fingers. "Mmm. I think I'd like s'more."

"Me too, only…" Padraig placed a hand on his belly and made a face like he'd eaten a sour green caterpillar.

"What's the matter, Padraig?"

"My tummy hurts a little bit. I wish we were home."

"No, no, we can't give up yet. You just have a touch of jungle fever. We should lie down again — to rest your tummy."

The boys lay down, just to rest, but instead they fell asleep.

"*MEeeeeeooooooOW!*" An alarming screech jolted them out of their dreams.

"Padraig, was that what I think it was?"

"Y-yes," Padraig whispered. "A baby leopard."

"*MEeeeeeooooooOW!*"

"By juniper! There it is again," said Roger. "I think it needs help."

"Really?" Padraig squeaked. "I think it needs its mum."

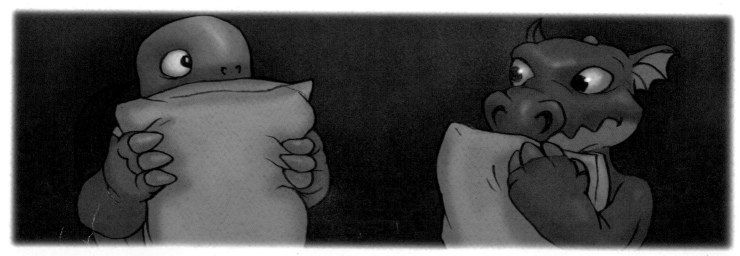

Roger searched the tent for his flashlight. "Padraig, my friend, the mummy leopard is obviously detained. It is time for us to be courageous."

"It is? But I thought the goal was to stay in the tent all night and see the animals in the morning. No one said anything about rescues."

"If we're brave enough to stay out all night, then we're brave enough to rescue a leopard."

"*MEeeeeeoooooooOW!*"

Roger unzipped the tent and shone his flashlight into the dark jungle. "We must save the lost leopard, Padraig."

Padraig hopped up. "Very well, if you insist. Perhaps it is a very little lost leopard."

"That's the spirit!" Roger thumped his friend on the back and stepped through the tent flap.

Roger swung the flashlight this way and that, peering into the dense jungle.

"See anything?" Padraig asked.

"It could be anywhere—trapped in a vine or caught in a log or squeezed in the coils of a boa constrictor."

Padraig shivered. "Let's find it quick."

"MEeeeeeeoooooooOW!"

The sound came from directly above the boys. Roger shone the light into the branches of a tall tree and saw a kitten—er, leopard.

"Thar she blows!" cried Padraig.

"That's not how you say it," said Roger.

"Then what am I supposed to say?"

"I've spotted the quarry!" Roger called.

"Of course it's spotted," said Padraig. "It's a leopard."

But just as Roger fixed the beam on the kitten-er-leopard, the flashlight fizzled out with a pop. The two boys stood in the dark.

"MEeeeeeeeeeoooooooooooOW!"

"Now what are we going to do?" asked Roger.

"I don't know," Padraig said. The dragon sucked in his breath and blew out a tiny flame.

Roger put his hands on his hips. "Have you always been able to do that?"

"No." Padraig's flame went out, plunging the boys back into darkness. "Usually I just puff a little smoke when I hiccup."

"Do you think you could do it again?"

"I could give it a try. Want me to?"

"I do."

Padraig blew a flame while Roger searched the tree again. When they found the kitten-er-leopard, Padraig flew up to help while Roger talked them down one step at a time.

The kitten-er-leopard gave both Padraig and Roger a lick, then scampered away to find its mum.

"Do you think it needs any more help?" Padraig asked.

"Indeed not, my good man," said Roger. "We have done a noble deed, and now it's time for rest."

"Besides," said Padraig, "a baby leopard is one thing, but a big mother leopard is quite another."

"Just so!" agreed Roger.

Roger and Padraig returned to their tent, but no matter how much they yawned and wiggled, they couldn't get to sleep.

"Do you think it will ever be morning?" Padraig wondered. "The nights sure are long at Mount Sillymanborrow."

Roger looked at his friend's unhappy frown. "We could always go back to home base."

Padraig sighed. "But we wanted to spend the whole night."

"Don't worry," Roger said. "We can try again."

The boys climbed out of their tent and headed home.

"What about our gear?" Padraig asked.

"We can come back for it tomorrow," said Roger.
"And I can tell you the Sillymanborrow story."

"Yes, indeed. Tomorrow is another day." Padraig pointed to the sunrise. "Today! It's morning. We spent the whole night outside!"

"By my galloping ancestors, you're right!" exclaimed Roger. "It's morning, and we great adventurers are ready for more."

"More adventure!"

"More excitement!"

"More fun!"

"After a nap." Roger yawned. "I think brave explorers take naps."

"Jolly good," said Padraig. "And then breakfast?"

Roger yawned again. "Yes, indeed."

The Legend of Mount Sillymanborrow

Long ago a man lived at the bottom of a great hill. One morning he decided to make waffles for his breakfast.

"I don't have any flour," he said. "I'll go to my neighbor Sam and ask if I might borrow some."

He left his home and went east, then north, then west, and then south until he came to Sam's house. He asked to borrow the flour, and Sam gladly lent it. The man took the flour and went home, going north, east, south, and then west.

A long, long journey.

After he poured the flour and baking powder into the bowl, he discovered he had no milk. "Alas," he said, "another long, long journey."

He left his house and headed east. But after only a few yards, he passed his own barn and heard, "Moo!"

"Aha!" he exclaimed. He milked his cow and took the full pail back to the kitchen. He stirred some milk into the bowl.

He then discovered he had no eggs. He sighed. "One more trip to see Sam."

The man left his unfinished batter and started east again toward the morning sun, which had risen quite high in the sky. But as he crossed his yard, he heard a cackling from his own chicken coop.

"Aha!" He hopped in the air, changed directions, and went to gather eggs. Back in his kitchen, he realized he was very hungry indeed. He mixed the batter, but when it was ready, he made another discovery. He had no waffle iron.

"Surely there are no waffle irons in my barn or in my chicken coop. But Sam will have one."

The man went out his front door, walked east, then turned north, then west, then south.

Sam willingly lent him the waffle iron, and the man trudged home.

Another long, long journey.

Back home, the man got to work. "I shall have to eat my waffles for lunch instead of breakfast," he said.

When he placed his stack of waffles on the table, a knock rattled his door. He opened the door to find Sam standing there with a bottle of syrup in his hand.

"I thought the waffles would be done by now," Sam said, "and you would need the syrup."

"Come in, come in," said the man. "Did you happen to bring butter?"

"No," Sam said.

"Oh dear, the waffles will be cold by the time you go all the way home and return."

"I don't think so." Sam trotted down the porch steps, across the man's yard, going west to his own home. In a minute, he was back with butter and a jug of apple juice. "Let's eat," he said.

The two sat down to a waffle breakfast eaten at noon and enjoyed by both the good neighbor and the silly man.